MW01712987

The Rebellious Slave

Breaking the Matrix

Mike Bhangu

BBP

ISBN 978-1-988735-28-3 (pbk.) — ISBN 978-1-988735-29-0 (ebook)

Illustrator: Mike Bhangu
Published by BB Productions
British Columbia, Canada
thinkingmanmike@gmail.com

I dedicate this manuscript to all the unknown thinkers of the world.

Table of Contents

Preface
Introduction

Disillusioned
Escape from Nimh
Daydreamer
The New Age Feudal System
Artificial Suffering
Mind Tricks
In the Wind I Blow an Innocent Kiss
I Challenge
Our First Mother
Citizen of the Natural World: Worldian
Manufactured
A Top-Down Problem
To Be Rich
Fancy Eggs
Bred this Way
Master or Servant
The Machine and Me
Built like This
Ground Zero
Skipping Rocks
False Living
Individuality
Starry-Eyed
Natural Selections
Like an Island
Circumstances
A Curse or a Blessing?
Happiness
Under Attack is the Happy Me
To Mimic
Me

An Unbiased Mind
Raindrops
Trolls of Suffering and Pain
Born Pure
Stick and Stone
The Army of the Social Activist
The Good Citizen
The New World: A Flower in February
How to Change the World
Age of the Aquarian
Why Him?
The New Romans We Be
Adam Smith's Side-Effect
Caged
Trouble
Your Unique Life Purpose
Stardust in my Shoes
The Same Caste
Immortal Me
Lagoon
The Invisible Leeching-Effect
Salt
Fragrance and Thorns
Kismet and Me
South Paw
The Changing of Guard

Preface

The Rebellious Slave is a collection of independent entries taken from my notebook—those I made while on the journey to discover the self and the worlds around me. Together, they present a different way of viewing the world, popular ideas, and an individual's place amid them. My hope is that the alternative perspective I present will motivate others to reevaluate why they want what they want, why they know what they know, and why they believe what they believe. I wish to inspire because the manner in which a person's mind is trained, and the substance readily available to the mind, cages an individual to an untrue reality.

The articles within were written individually and then brought together to create a manuscript. Although a sense of transition is worked in, the expressions should be read within this context. Moreover, *The Rebellious Slave* is the extended version of *I am Mouse*.

Introduction

Well, here I am… I did a little star gazing so to separate the mortal and the immortal me, and I did a little star gazing so to understand the world I was thrust into. And after years of staring at the night canvas, I've come to realize that I was born into a world, as you were, already in motion, and to set beliefs, agendas, power struggles, and as a member of the ruled class.

Society can be divided into two dominant groups, the rulers and the ruled. The philosophical expressions within this manuscript attempt to briefly address the deficiencies in the rule of shepherds, and the feelings of those they herd.

The Rebellious Slave presents notions many people have considered, at one time or another, or were troubled by, but for one or more reasons, these ideas didn't receive an audience. I guess the world is occasionally too fast paced and people might not have the energy and time to travel outside the box and audit their thoughts. Hopefully, this is where my work can help. Perhaps, my thoughts can revitalize yours.

....

Years of thought accumulated. Broken and rebuilt in the process. Transfer I do through the fingertips. And my hope is that these ideas provide you with a good starting point from which to seek, and if need be, I hope you find hope and absorb it like me.

A mountain is a hill.
A mouse is a lion.

Disillusioned

The ones who know me can't understand why I haven't made the earthly gains my strengths predicted. They sometimes look at me as if I threw away my earthly talents. What words can I write to them to describe my disposition?

My design is capable of thriving in a consumer society, but sometimes my design influences my thoughts to detach from the secular pulls of a consumer's living, and sometimes my thoughts wander into places a capitalist should not be.

I'm not sure why my design allows for this. Perhaps, the parts combined together to make me slipped through the quality assurance checkpoints faulty. Perhaps, there's more to our human condition than just material wishes. Whatever the reason, the consequences are typically the same, my secular ambitions silence and the beliefs they stem from hibernate—meaning that my wants change and my thoughts release themselves from the popular purposes given by the machine.

Luckily, detachment isn't random and I only detach when there's a challenge—a dispute from within and a quarrel provoked by an outside stimulant. When challenged, the chemistry of my brain and the parameters of my mind's eye change. Unused pathways open, dead information resurrects, and the information that best interacts with a world built by a shepherd-less ego slowly silences. In the end, what's popular transforms into something foreign, new beliefs and wants surface, and the machine's pull weakens.

When provoked, the information that surfaces typically triggers my cognitive condition to act more collective. The information encourages attributes as empathy, compassion, peace, and unconditional love to influence thoughts and actions. Under such internal inductions, it's easy to detach from the pulls of the consumer culture and the mind state of a capitalist.

Again, detachment isn't random. However, detachment is readily stimulated. Almost every day something causes my mind to detach.

- Sometimes it's the irrational and artificial cost to live and the low wages given.

- Sometimes it's the infant's purchasing power coupled with a pay-cheque-to-pay-cheque existence.

- Sometimes it's the regression of the middle-class and their transformation into middle-class peasants.

- Sometimes it's the single parent attempting to balance on a line of credit.

- Sometimes it's the products designed to breakdown after a given period.

- Sometimes it's the inaccurate history written by the empires, religions, kings, priests, and colonialists.

- Sometimes it's the genetic modification of our food supply and corporate mass pollution.

- Sometimes it's the underdeveloped value system nurtured by our popular culture and the expense of a good education.

- Sometimes it's the politicians who forget to represent the needs of the common person.

- And sometimes it's the comparison of a life-long mortgage, and a rental living, to the feudal system memorialized by the European Dark Ages.

I'm with the earthly talents to rise as a capitalist, but in a manufactured world that prevents a higher standard of awareness, the "humanitarian me" is encouraged to speak. When the human in me is needling my mind's eye, it's impossible to think of only selfish gains and material accumulation. Perhaps I'll be forgiven in heaven for the difference, but until the day of my judgment or until the built world changes, I have little choice but to exercise my talents to repair the unnatural damage. With paper and pen, I take my place amid the dead and step onto the battlefield.

My beliefs and my wants are not the same as popular thought—those built inside the box. Mine, built and born outside, are known to throw uppercuts.

I don't want to live and die a lie. So I sacrifice. I try. I live against the wind and pretend to fly.

We've culturally evolved to think that the degenerations of our everyday living are true and unchangeable. At the same time, we've evolved to believe that we're at the peak of human existence. I ask—Does anyone else feel a contradiction between the two claims? Unless of course, the peak of humanity includes degenerate things.

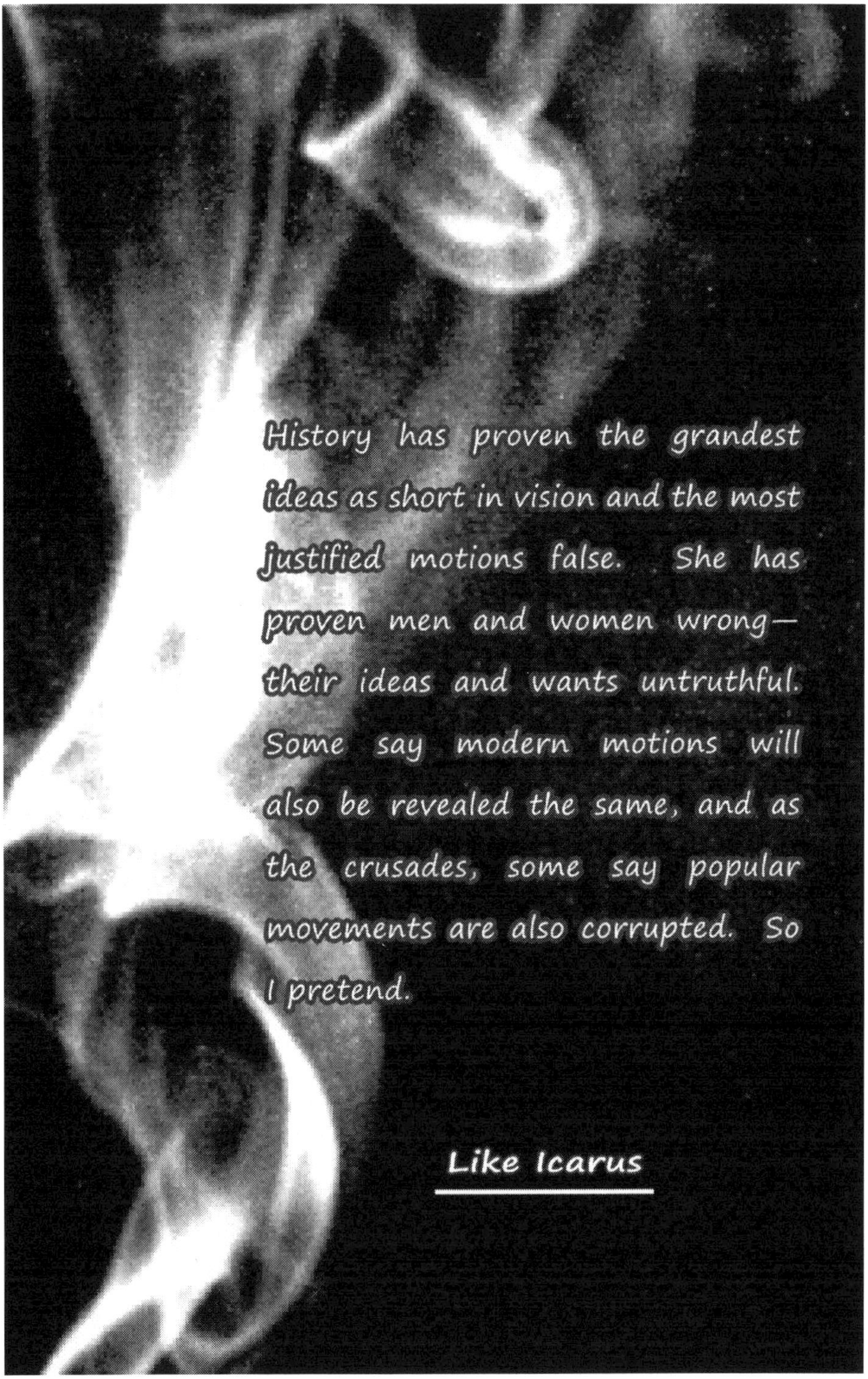

History has proven the grandest ideas as short in vision and the most justified motions false. She has proven men and women wrong—their ideas and wants untruthful. Some say modern motions will also be revealed the same, and as the crusades, some say popular movements are also corrupted. So I pretend.

Like Icarus

Escape from Nimh

> *Not too long ago, I set about examining the value system the manmade world influenced me to incubate. After opening it up and taking a closer look, to my surprise, I discovered it was virtually empty. The revelation was shattering. I felt like a squirrel that spent the entire summer gathering nuts to only realize, come winter, that the nutshells were empty.*
>
> *So, I did what any rebel would. I turned my hat to the back, assumed the position of the thinking man, and rebuilt my cognitive content. Today, I am a champion like "Money May" but of the consciousness.*

Answer me this my fellow humans—Are we really on this earth to work an eight-hour shift, to have the productions of our blood and labour taken, to live pay-cheque-to-pay-cheque while balancing on a line of credit, to give forty years to a mortgaged existence, to sweat for the system when the financial chains will remain regardless, and to thirst strictly for the weekends?

Answer me this my fellow humans—Are we really on this earth to have our minds bombarded by the agenda of governments and big corporations, to continually have our subconscious and our decision-making process influenced by engineered information, to have our awareness placed within a box so we'll stay as screws for the system, and to constantly want an escape from Nimh?

Please, fill me in. Is this some sort of punishment, and how much of the system is God-sent? And, if you or I make a break as the rats did, will there be divine consequence?

A question for the ears of the Universe—Without a million in a bank account or buried in the backyard, isn't it cruel to birth a child? I only ask this because, at times, it seems as if life is given to a servant, born to suffer and struggle—all in the name of satisfying the system. Born to parents without large amounts of cash, a child only grows to repeat the same cycle that chains most parents—to work until grey and weak, to consume without need, to be told what to do and think, to sacrifice the spirit for material things, to pay an irrational price, and to bear the title "debt-slave".

It would appear, at times, that the only thing most people give life to is a screw for the system, destined to endure, and this in so-called developed nations. The right to raise a child correctly is stolen by our artificial and destitute eco-political conditions. Escape I want from this experiment. Escape I want for myself and those yet to receive a body dependent. Is it possible to rewrite our social contract, or are these truly the best gifts we can leave tomorrow's children?

North America was meant to be the New World. A land envisioned as a place for the common person to live free of the corrupt influences perpetuated by the Old. And in the beginning, that was probably so, but on the contemporary scene, the Old World has infiltrated the New. Those who rule are again manipulating and exploiting the general public so to reinforce the status of the few. The bewildered herd must be controlled and society is structured to keep the people senselessly occupied and trapped as the ruled. Escape from Nimh I wish for, as those who braved the New World not too long ago, but where to go? The Old are the masters of almost all.

Under the setting of the Old World, most people existed for the benefit of the wealthiest, and the structure of society, including the beliefs taught to the general public, were designed to reinforce the power of that group. But the contemporary person doesn't know what was meant by the term, and with few to defend the vision of a New World, the Old attitude slowly seeped back into the picture. Understand my friend, civilization is taking steps backward.

…learn the language, make a break, and rebuild.

Through public policy, we can journey down a road less traveled. Through public policy, we can remedy the many problems. But first, public policy should be written to serve the public. Regrettably, the politicians fiddle while we, the new Romans, slowly turn to ashes.

Innumerable faces were deceived to believe that something higher there be. But regardless of the time put in, the invisible chains will remain until death. Only a tiny percentage of the population can escape the artificial financial circumstances that restrict relative freedom of consciousness. The passing of every generation appears to provide the evidence. A lesson to repeat or a lesson to question?

Daydreamer

Question I do the eight-hours, the five-days, and the before and the after extorted by the built world. In total, more than eight-hours a day are given to a pay-cheque-to-pay-cheque existence and a line of credit. By the time the mind is free of its occupation, the mind has little time and energy to develop the other aspects of the human condition. That is, after the completion of all the daily material household and family responsibilities without end.

Now, you'd think those who give the majority of their life to the built world might be able to escape a pay-cheque-to-pay-cheque existence and a line of credit, but a reality this isn't. Most people are unable to break through to experience relative financial freedom, and too many can't secure the resources required to sustain the self for longer than a two-week period.

Pay-cheque-to-pay-cheque most people live and the tragedy is yet to end. In their desire to do more than exist, many have little choice but to work jobs that don't bring them happiness. Instead, inside the mind, they fight the self for over eight-hours a day, for over five-days a week, and for over forty-years.

And why do they war with themselves? They fight to understand why their happiness must be bargained in exchange for life. They fight to understand the financial chains that annually thicken. They fight to find a just reason for their disposition. They fight to suppress their discontentment in hopes to one-day taste relative financial freedom. And until they turn old and grey they fight.

They fight, and they fight, and they fight. And oddly, they fight thinking their fight is natural, they fight thinking the Universe designed their struggles, and they fight to over-pay for certain things they have a natural right to.

I ask—Can this truly be the height of living for everyone or is it the height of life for those born rich? Think on it. Who truly benefits from the contemporary system and the neo-liberal ideology that fuels it? Who truly lives with relative financial freedom and happiness? Please, someone fill me in. I thought the free market wasn't designed to enslave the people of a nation.

....

The majority of a person's wake time is fed to the system. Life is exchanged for life, and in the deal, the mind is allocated little time to develop a greater awareness. Nine-to-five daydreaming is what most people have left.

Tell me—What's the meaning of giving over eight-hours a day, five-days a week, and forty-years when the chains will remain regardless? If anything, subjecting the mind to the lifestyle of a servant will only cause the chains to thicken and further wean the mind from purposes with purpose. When this happens, the eight-hours, the five-days, and the forty-years will inconspicuously turn into a lifelong prison sentence.

People are sheep and the wool is their sweat. But unlike the four-legged creatures, the person is daily shaven. It would seem that actual sheep have it better than the human.

My hopes came. My dreams passed. The darkness set in. In the dark I stand. Is my birth to blame? Give me a name. Something I can become—something more than just a servant of the system.

The New Age Feudal System

This idea of a life-long mortgage doesn't make sense. Why? Well, my life is worth more than half an acre with a structure on it. Without hesitation, I'm willing to give a decade. Perhaps then enough youth with remain to experience the one life and the one world.

Since we're on the topic, the similarities between the contemporary system and the system of the Feudal Age can't be missed. During the Feudal Age, the majority of the people had little choice but to work the land of their liege so as to live. In return, they typically received shelter from the elements and protection from roving bands of thieves and mercenaries. However, if the peasants were unable to work for whatever reason, their shelter was taken from them. The same is true with the system we have. If an individual, with a mortgage, can't work for some time and make the monthly payments, they'll most likely lose their home. If living in a rental, the removal is much quicker.

This idea of a life-long mortgage doesn't make sense. Why? Well, my life is worth more than half an acre with a structure on it. Without hesitation, I'm willing to give a decade. Perhaps then enough youth with remain to experience the one life and the one world.

Perhaps I lost my senses. Maybe I tripped and bumped my head against the ivory tower and knocked myself unconscious. Or perhaps this is the nuance of the infamous. Or maybe this is the plight of the good-hearted. To learn the reasons why the Feudal Age has resurfaced, please read *Distracted and Defeated.*

No matter the color, sex, or creed, most people are "debt-slaves". This is so because wages are too low and the cost to live is too high. Fortunately, both happenings are manmade and they can be eliminated by those who lead. But the ruling class understand a debt as an invisible chain, and a chained individual is easier to control than one who roams the land freely.

The contemporary economy gives hopes and dreams but without ways and means.

Tell me—What's the meaning behind working so hard when the pay-off is absent—What's the point when the system doesn't respect the human condition—What's the meaning when the irrational cost to living forces a person to live pay-cheque-to-pay-cheque?

The rich are the only who progress. The rest regress. The poor become poorer, and the middle-class transform into middle-class peasants. It feels as if the system has either evolved to undress itself of its human component or that component was never a part of the system. Nothing else can explain the servitude.

Artificial Suffering

The financial hardships most people struggle under are interpreted as unchangeable, as the power of the sun over a snowflake. However, the phenomenon is unnatural, as a genetically modified seed. As such, it can be changed. It's foolish to think otherwise.

The environment is sick and the organisms dependent on the environment naturally reflect.

History is a continuous battle between "the haves" and "the have-nots". No matter if "the have-nots" know or not. No matter if "the have-nots" have their heads in the sand.

Mind Tricks

Every generation is born unaware of what is and what was, and those born tomorrow won't know of the past or the present if not taught.

Born to high fuel prices, lofty housing costs, low wages, a life on credit, and on and on, a person will grow assuming that all the mentioned are natural, as the seas or stars, and the suffering attached as a fact of life and unchangeable. Under this impression, few will attempt to eliminate the problems. Under this illusion, people will interpret the short chains that prevent the becoming of the ideal human being as a design of the Universe and her unbreakable principles.

Tricked are the unborn and little is done by the living to improve the built world they'll grow to uphold. Can this be because far too many are distracted from higher meaning and unable to see a better reality?

Every generation is born unaware of what is and what was, and generations born tomorrow won't know if not taught. Hold on... teach if that's all you can, but if the fire in you is strong, effort to give tomorrow's children the positives by smashing the negatives. Then teach them of the countless sacrifices required to free their minds from their otherwise soon-to-be mephistophelian torment.

....

The book, *A Beautiful Destruction*, provides greater detail to the eco-political hardships alluded to. It also presents academic research to support the expressions within this manuscript.

We must think of the next. If we refuse to, the future faces will reside on a shipwreck. To this effect, most folks in the know are afraid to stand toe-to-toe with the causes of human suffering. I think they might be afraid of losing their material holdings, or they fail to recognize death as the greatest end. My stance is a little different: If all is lost, let it be for a greater cause. Ashes to ashes. This because death will steal it regardless.

In the Wind I Blow an Innocent Kiss

Even though the modern mind doesn't truly care for how the world will function tomorrow, this generation will still be remembered as responsible. You see, the world left for the unborn will be the world they'll grow to know and why wouldn't they hold us responsible.

But mesmerized by the shadows cast inside Plato's Cave, the modern mind doesn't seem to care. Lost to fantasies and to material things, the person is distracted from cocooning higher meaning.

The mind is distracted and preoccupied with fantasies and material things, and when it's not this, the mind is kept busy working towards or thinking about meeting the body's basic needs, making payments, paying taxes, living pay-cheque-to-pay-cheque, and all of the other artificial economic catalysts that distract and preoccupy the conscious and subconscious.

It's no secret and the human being is born without wants, beliefs, and knowledge—a person becomes what he or she experiences and learns. This said, the value system the contemporary built world influences a person to develop encourages fantasies, material things, and the irrational cost to live to occupy top-of-mind awareness, and the desire for a better world doesn't carry the same cognitive presence.

Tricked and caged is the mind's awareness, and little time and energy are given to questions such as—How can the world be a better place and what can I do to improve her condition?

To add to the illusion, outside the built world, the means to secure an individual's basic needs are next to nil. The machine controls almost all worldly resources and streams of production and distribution. What this means is, if a person wishes to live, an individual has no place else to go and the human condition can't realistically escape how the machine shapes an individual's value system.

Knowing this, it's difficult to blame a person for their lack of action. Knowing this, it's difficult to blame the human for acting as an island. But even then this generation can never truly outrun the fact that they'll be remembered as responsible. This generation is leaving behind a damaged world that'll raise the children of tomorrow.

Knowingly or unknowingly, by participating without objecting, a person gives their consent. By participating without objecting, a person enlarges in influence the wrong and allows it to grow in size and strength. Coincidentally, giving the impression that the wrong is natural and constant.

Even though the modern mind doesn't truly care for how the world will function tomorrow, this generation will still be remembered as responsible. You see, the world left for the unborn will be the world they'll grow to know and why wouldn't they hold us responsible.

An allegory designed by Plato to illustrate the notion that what is actually isn't. In it, he describes a group of people chained from head to toe inside a cave, with a fire to their back, and able to see only the shadows projected by the fire. Born chained in the cave, the only knowledge of reality is the knowledge they've gathered from the shadows on the cave wall. With this knowledge, they build their values, wants, beliefs, etc. Unfortunately, the true reality isn't the shadows but the causes of the shadows, and the chained people are unable to see the causes. The only way they'll be able to see the causes is if they break the chains that restrict them from turning around.

The little ones are translations, and not knowing what a human is, the little ones are silent victims—born to a world that takes advantage of their ignorance—born to a world that conditions a consumer's intelligence.

I Challenge

I do not challenge the entire establishment. I only challenge the parts and the beliefs of the machine that shackle the wrists and the ankles.

We are chained insofar as the person naturally translates the environments, and the built world doesn't allow the many to breakthrough and experience relative financial freedom.

Now, this isn't to say that the whole of the built world is backward. On paper, the system has never been as educated or as politically, socially, economically, and technologically advanced. The built world has never had the potential that the contemporary scene has.

I do not challenge the entire establishment. I only challenge the parts and the beliefs of the machine that shackle the wrists and the ankles.

Those who laid the foundation to the contemporary built world, so many generations ago, created the circumstances that would enhance their demographics influence, wealth, and power, and not an environment able to increase the living standards of the general public. Today, that intention is more than apparent, and the evidence includes the demonic cost to live, the 40-hours a week of breath stolen, a life on credit, and a lifelong mortgage.

The Second World War saw the destruction of the old world order, and in nations such as America and Canada, the people rose to guide government. Under this aura of influence, historical gains were taken—social, political, and economical. However, these gains are under attack. This might be because the people forgot their status prior to WW2. Unintentionally, the people permit a reversal.

The private sector should not control the contemporary basics or the economy, and by extension, the person. It's like asking a hungry shark to watch over a school of fish.

Our First Mother

Ignorance is abundant. Born dependent, people have forgotten. Too many pretend as if she's a mere inanimate object. Ergas omnes (*"a crime against all"*).

And how to hold them responsible? They were bred by our popular culture ignorant, and they were born unaware of who first became pregnant.

Or perhaps they're the Anti-Christ divided. Its energy spread through billions and our First Mother cries. On behalf of them I summit. On behalf of them I apologize. On behalf I identify, stick, move, and try.

Black-eyed and bruised, I see two holders of hope, two ultra-power agents within every nation—Governments and Corporations. They're with the technology. They're with the means. Like knights in shining armour, they're capable of bringing mass change.

Governments and Corporations have the power to change the things in need of change, but unfortunately, they sometimes behave as our First Mother's enemy and the dividers of us and our first family.

Although the two prefer to blame the people and their habits, they're the makers of the destruction and the pollution. You see, they're the gods of the consumer culture, the machines, and the products that injure. They're the cause of the oil spills, the clear-cuts, and the polluted raindrops. They are, they are, they are the reason. Killers of her speechless children like the ozone, the panda bear, and the rainforest.

But how to hold them responsible? Giants they are and only a man I am. Even if a million of me there were, they can easily avert any attempt.

Of the two, only the built world will try and manipulate you.

There are two worlds, the natural and the built. Until the two vibrations become one, both worlds will continue to cause the human condition suffering.

Citizen of the Natural World: Worldian

The people are synthetically separated from their First Mother. No matter, beyond all of woman and man's designs, we belong to what is forever truthful, never fallible. As you, I am a citizen of the natural world first. I am a Worldian.

Why? It's simple. The Universe created my earthly entity dependent on earthly things.

Besides, the designs that divide us were created by woman and man and not nature. They were designed by mortal creatures, creatures potentially fallible.

For those reasons, I give my allegiance to our First Mother before any destructive design of the built world.

Loyal I am to my First Mother, but unduly, the decision-makers do not and did not see the Earth in the same context. They did not see beyond themselves to know themselves and to comprehend the bigger picture. They do not understand themselves as children of our First Mother.

The contemporary world reflects their attitude. The manufactured information buries the natural and restricts a person from translating the information this realm holds. Far too many people didn't learn to love the natural world.

Perhaps that's why so many people attack the generations not yet born, and why so many people destroy the natural world that rightfully belongs to the future. Please appreciate that we have the power to influence what they'll grow to understand and to experience, and it would appear that we prefer they translate a dead planet.

Even in pollution, the greedy will find profit. The system creates the pollution and the system we have will find a way to profit from it. The system isn't geared to remedy the problem but exploit it. At the rate that we're going, who knows, maybe one-day they'll bottle air and put a price tag on it. Think about it, they already bottle water and sell it.

The subconscious influences a person to alter their conscious mind state. This because the human and the natural world are not one. The lack of harmony causes suffering and the subconscious reacts by requesting an escape from this reality.

Manufactured

Pollution
Murderous teardrops
Dying dirt

Unnatural truths
Like raindrops on a windshield
Easily removed

We've turned. We've turned on our beginnings. We've turned to hurt the Mother of all earthly things, such as the seas, trees, lions, leaves, penguins, people, and chimpanzees. Dematerialized, we are forever family, including even fire, ice, and flying things.

I can see a maniac and you can see him too. Look for the constructed person in the mirror. Do you see the consumer as I see you?

The world can be a better place. The problems that plague are manmade. However, the people able to elevate human living, those few with the resources, influence, technology, time, and power, are preoccupied with something else, or they benefit from the status quo. Nothing else can explain their lack of action. Or perhaps, they lack the vision. If the latter is correct, the solution is simple, read my work. But if the former is so, which I think is true, then there is little hope for the common people. Unless of course, God intervenes and pushes the reset button to this video game called life. Or the people affected by the backwardness mobilize and retake their natural rights.

A Top-Down Problem

The machine might be broken. Top down and trickling down, the machine forgot to communicate angelic information. Shockingly, it sometimes communicates the opposite. The machine even managed to corrupt many CEOs, preachers, bankers, and politicians.

One too many CEOs, preachers, bankers, and politicians are corrupt, and they present a top-down problem. More importantly, what did they expect, the people below not to imitate and not to compromise the integrity of the soul for selfish ends. If the individuals who lead readily forget to love the soul, and if the people who lead readily behave crooked, naturally, those who follow will mimic.

I Follow Thee...

I follow thee if thee be a truthful thing. Lead me with humility. I follow thee. I follow thee if thee be heart-strong like me. Lead me my philosopher king. I follow thee.

I'm willing to surrender, and I'm willing to give my sovereignty to another. Until my last breath, I'm willing to follow ideas greater.

To Be Rich

All bridges behind me are in ashes. The end of the Earth can be seen in the distance. There's a nickel and a dime in my pocket. And my shoes are missing pieces. To make the quest a little more hopeless, my stone grew legs last night and started running. In the confusion, I tripped and fell on my stick, and since it was thin, the break was instant.

Seemingly a curse, the poor are often blessed with thoughts kind. But what's the worth of moral ideas if they're trapped in mind? You see, grand ideas are heavenly and man manifests in mind, and unnaturally, the DNA of the built world has "Darwinized" to bind the kind.

To this end, the most privileged are blind. They deny the divine parts of the mind. They play in agreement with their own selfish design. With nothing grand in mind they climb.

If they had developed a kind mind, the type that reminds the "I" of another's consciousness, they would remedy the unnatural happenings that harm the person—degenerations such as the destructive production methods, genetic modifications, disposable economics, and corrupt political practices. If they had developed a kind mind, the world would not be as it is.

But they didn't and my stone is lost and my stick is broken. I've lost and broke my only means to challenge the unnatural degenerations that hinder human development. Yet, even if things were different, whom am I really fooling? Defy I could nothing. The god of greed is too strong? Or am I wrong? Can a common man defy the entire world?

In this lifetime, all I can do is ask the rich to access the divine mind—to use their influence, wealth, creativity, and knowledge of things to be kind queens and kings. If not for the sole reason of being the greatest of people, individuals akin to Solomon, Asoka, Jassa Singh, Cyrus, and the Great Gobind, then for their place amid the angels. The greater the power, the greater the prerequisite, and more is asked of them at the gates to Heaven.

....

Realistically another dream and the rich are often bred self-meaned.

Fancy Eggs

Dazzled by the fame and the wealth, we too often forget to examine before we bow and praise.

But I guess it isn't completely our fault, the famous and the wealthy present the self as a Fabergé Egg, and it's difficult not to be dazzled by the elegant design and expensive jewels. Unwittingly, and no thanks to big media that presents them as if they were God sent, we too often give far too much admiration to those who might not deserve it.

Dazzled by the elegance and the shine, we sometimes forget to consider what's inside the egg—we sometimes forget to question where the wealth and the fame originated from—we sometimes forget to consider what we're actually bowing to and praising.

Virtue or corruption—the light or the darkness—the angelic or the demonic, a choice is made when we admire those sullied by deceit and corruption and the choice is worsened when we know of the dirt that covers.

It's Okay to Have it All

It's okay to make a million, so long as the million didn't include another's suffering, known or unknown.

It's okay to wear gold and nice clothes, so long as the mind's master is the soul.

It's okay to strive toward a secular goal, so long as one is guided by the immortal.

It's okay to have wealth, power, and influence. It's okay to have it all.

Bred this Way

The angel of death courts democracy and the selfish seem to control all. Popular media sells sex and young adults buy. Money is created from thin air and interest is collected by greedy private enterprise. The marketing industry and the political machinery readily mix truths and lies. Corporations are Godless and they destroy natural life. The many are trapped to the lower levels and waiting under the table for the crumbs from the pie. And the cost to live grew wings and now touches the sky.

The artificial coupling between uncontrolled greed and the human being is destroying. The evidence is such that the power of the sun would be the appropriate metaphoric expression to describe it. But yet, the majority do little to peacefully defy and defend.

I guess it's easy not to care for that which isn't conditioned in thee. The person is designed to absorb information and translate. Our metaphysical and physical motions are predetermined by the value system learned from the environments. To this end, the norms conditioned by our popular reality influence people to ignore the happenings and to interpret them as unchangeable actualities.

We're bred this way, so, can we truly be blamed? I'm sure if we were taught differently, responsibility we would take. For now, the finger should be pointed at those who teach, like the masters of t.v. We are only human and born knowing near nothing.

Life in the Iron Age

The pillars that hold the sky in place might be nearing their breaking point, but as long as there are goods to consume, entertainment to occupy the downtime, and pleasurable inductions to experience, few will attempt to prevent the collapse. I must ask—Will we be forgiven by heaven for the ignorance?

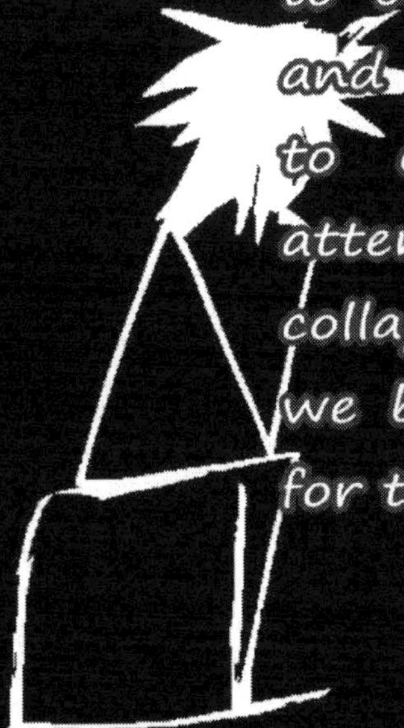

Master or Servant

It's an age-old phenomenon—the individual translating the environment, and in today's world, the environment has groomed the master as servant and alienated the "I" from knowing what it is to be the controller of beliefs, wants, and choices.

To be a master, a person must understand the nature of the mind and answer questions such as: Why do thoughts and wants occur? How do neural pathways develop? Why can neuron-to-neuron communications envelope? How can a state of mind be changed? How can stimulants impact thoughts? And how can a given environment nurture or neglect values?

A person must become more so to discover the nature of the master. Regrettably, the knowledge required to notice this isn't born with an individual. It must be learned and learn we do through our interactions with information.

To this end, the knowledge required to choose the master and slay the servant is missing. Popular information rarely communicates the required understanding, and instead, nurtures a value system that mostly maintains and enhances the status quo—a value system that assassinates the enlightened and encourages the birth of a distracted and preoccupied consumer. A limited awareness is catered. Yet, the knowledge exists and it's a matter of knowing where to look. In my search, I discovered higher understanding amid the great philosophers, poets, intellects, saints, and mystics of our past. Perhaps you might too.

....

Those who can, from time to time, stage-manage ideas, information, and knowledge. They do this to maintain and enhance the status quo. In this reality, an individual is unendingly misdirected by beliefs, wants, and expectations while the rulers remain the overlords. To learn more about this stratum, please read *Distracted and Defeated.*

Master or servant? The manmade world loves the second but tells the slave different.

A master is like a pilot. A slave is very much the opposite.

A master understands cause and effect. A slave's motions are fully determined.

A master understands how they become. A slave can't differentiate between the natural and the given.

A master understands why they want what they want. A slave understands this as much as a bee seeking pollen.

The Machine and Me

Like a Shakespearean tragedy, tragically, I was cast into an artificial realm that practices deliberate deception without the knowledge of what I be, how I be, and my natural information absorbing ability.

My birth and my growth, as yours, were entrusted to the builders of the manmade world. It was their responsibility to truthfully teach you and me about you and me. But instead, they betrayed us. I write this because far too many of the wants, beliefs, and "truths" they teach bring instability to the inner self and challenge the better half of the mind's essence. They create a distorted perception and trap my thoughts to a false narrative.

All this is a consequence, the machine built by the builders controls all aspects of life and it forgot to nurture an individual's entire essence. The prominent "truths" pushed are Darwinized ideas of accumulation, moral compromise, consumption, greed, violence, image, sensory pleasure, an entertained mind, and self-interest. These "truths" weren't meant to dominant. But instead, collectivity, contentment, benevolence, sharing, love, truth, humility, righteousness, virtue, and empathy were meant to reign.

Sometimes it feels as if we're restricted until death by these invisible chains of circumstance, inside a built world similar to "the Cave" Plato once described.

If this is a democracy, then the people are the masters of techniques and technologies. So, if we want more from human existence than to only consume things, the power lay in choosing.

Built like This

I was built like this, a chameleon in essence, and I naturally become my environments. To this extent—To be or not to be? Wait, let me rephrase. What be the thing I'm bred to be? The two conditions of my humanity, my invisible and my biology, take shape according to my realities, and regrettably, in a world built by shepherd-less egos, half of me hibernates.

Half of me searching for the divine man in me, and past the social contracts, it took several years to decode the innate in me, to see the chains, and to identify the mortal and the immortal me.

You see, the knowledge needed to please Thee was partially hidden from me. Instead, the popular knowledge did more to corrupt me and blind my mind to the eternal half in me. Instead, half empty I be.

Half empty I be and quick to be defeated. Unfortunately, it takes time for knowledge to manifest and become subconscious actions. Unfortunately, it takes time to separate the elements and interpret what is what and what is everlasting. Sometimes it takes a lifetime to defy the built world and become more than mere mortal, and to grow to know and hold the soul of an angel.

So please, burn the parts of the built world that roiled me if smoke is what you wish to see. I ask to let be to become and separate the water from the coloring—the dye cast by ahistorical thought and reality.

Under them I am and climbing. Bruised a bit but still dreaming. Short of breath but still breathing.

....

The mindset should be adjusted so the "I" can see its place within the body fortress. Perhaps then, together, we might ask with true purpose, what is our truest purpose?

But spiritual development is in direct contradiction with industrialism, the contemporary market, and the consumer culture. It's in conflict because it threatens profit. If an individual valued spiritual progress more than the consumption of the material and the senses, the money-makers would make less money. Not only this, the general public might demand more from their leaders—more God oriented behaviour.

I am not who I was. I will be not who I am. Who will be judged when my judgement day come? I am only human and subject to change as a chameleon. Place me in a benevolent environment and I will be righteous. Trap me to the darkness and witness a shallow grin.

Born in today's world as free as free can be but free I'll never be. I was born to a world that feeds purposeless purposes, gives meaningless knowledge, blinds the mind's eye, and instils feelings of moral discomfort.

Ground Zero

Who should be blamed for the situation that we're in, the person or the contemporary built world that teaches and coerces the person?

The situation that I refer to is the moral degradation of advanced civilizations, and since nothing can change the fact that the human condition is a near translation, I guess it only makes sense to point the finger at the built world and those who built it.

Just as an infection of the body needs the right environment to live, conditions must exist for any degeneration to exist, and the manmade world harbours these conditions.

To add to the entrapment, as the generations translate, reflect, and contribute to the built world, the structural conditions and the value system that nurture the moral corruption will continue to grow as generations grow to contribute. Like a cycle strengthening every time it cycles through.

If something isn't done, eventually, the generations to come will interpret the darkness as something natural, as a cloud, and a permanent fixture within the house that God built.

....

Top down and trickling down, popular media forgets to communicate angelic information. If you would like to learn more about the occurrences, please read *Angel vs. Demon*.

Paranoid by the time God allocated to me. Institutionalized by my society. I'm asking questions in the hope the answers free me. Please, don't forget about me. Forgive me. I'm only searching for the divine man in me.

The body is only a mud brick temple. As all will agree, the body is built to crumble. The soul is more. The soul is immortal. The soul is why I live. The soul is why I endure.

Skipping Rocks

Last night was a good night. I saw the sun bow, the moon take its place, and the stars slow-dancing on the middle of the lake. Last night was a good night. It allowed my thoughts to travel and enjoy a good conversation at the foot of a lake.

Last night was a good night. Why? Because modern communities prescribe a good conversation as a difficult commodity to come by. Many conversations rarely travel outside the popular culture and the different forms of artificial distractions such as money, sensory pleasure, and misinformation. And when it isn't any of the mentioned, conversations typically entertain what a person has, where a person travelled, what a person saw, how many beers a person drank, the different ways the ego was stroked, another's misfortune, provoked emotions, and the latest of the latest and not of ideas greater than the self.

In these types of conversations, people verbally flex, and mysteriously, they act as if these conversations are required to live like lungs filled with breath.

Perhaps in their mind's eye they believe the "I" is something more than mortal. Or it might be that the "I" is unaware of how the "I" becomes. Tell me—Why else would the "I" shape its mind to allow for the dissonance, and why else would the "I" verbally strut as if the Master of the Universe, or the Queen of an invisible castle, when most people are in the same boat?

Without prejudice. I must confess. Far too many conversations lack substance and the truth is very much subjective. But I guess this all makes sense. The built world conditions beliefs, ideas, wants, expected behaviour, and purposes without pretext. It's difficult to break through the context. I wonder—What would be of us if we were more than human—more than a reflection of the information experienced and absorbed from the world around us? Wait, that's not the right question.

Let me try again. What would be of use if those with the power to teach taught a higher standard of thinking?

Last night was a good night. It was a good night because I participated in a good conversation. I thought about the natural role of a corporation; the responsibility of a government to her children; the attack on our First Mother and her inhabitants; the purpose of nurturing ideas such as truth, love, humility, and compassion; and a people united to achieve a greater end.

Last night was a good night but also unfortunate. Regrettably, the dead were the only with anything of importance to communicate. Yet, they couldn't elaborate on their written thoughts to interact with my voice to create a new perspective—it was a one way conversation. Yet, imagine the likes of Rousseau and me skipping rocks by the lake. I wonder if he would be amazed... amazed to see women and men living past their 80s, 50 storey buildings, airplanes, and Escalades? I wonder if he would still be in awe after eaves-dropping on a conversation between a few friends?

....

The degenerations of modern living are not a mystery. The smoke can be seen in the distance. Mournfully, the mind has grown insensitive to it and thoughts are preoccupied with verbally flexing.

One is One until it's two. A distinction there is only between the Heaven-oriented and the fool.

False Living

A consumer's beliefs and wants are purposely limited and the consumer is unaware of this—they're designed to encourage a person to want what the market creates and nothing more or less.

To make matters worse, contemporary products cater to human weakness—the reason for their self-determination. Unaware, the right to the highest state of realization is kept away from the human and a consumer unknowingly operates with a limited perception.

Most people are too busy chasing. Too busy is the space and time in the place of thinking. Little room is left for higher living and too many people are preoccupied by unnecessary needing—real needs never fully breeding, like true freedom, true happiness, true belonging, the "true me," and true peace.

Constitutional public policy is unwilling to hear this. Afraid they are of the economic consequence. The system might regress or collapse and too egoist are the elitists to allow a relapse. We, the new Romans, are burning.

Please understand that people truthfully informed about their place in the world will consume less, and consuming less will improve one's metaphysical happiness. However, this might reduce the influence of the powers that be and the giants can't allow this.

Most people might know this if public policy showed it, but those with the pen to ink a nation's direction are minions of the market.

HE BOUGHT
HE SOLD
HE LOST
HE FOUND

The manner in which we were trained by the built world is only one of the options available to us. But oddly, we've fixated ourselves and pretend as if there is no other method. As such, a consumer is the height of the human.

The thinking gene is neglected. The built world isn't nurturing this aspect of a person. Can it be that if the trend continues, the thinking gene will evolve as dormant?

Individuality

The idea of an individual, who makes autonomous decisions, is a myth but it's presented as an absolute so to misdirect.

If you don't believe me, answer this—What's so unique about absorbing information that every mind uses, to create wants and motions? It's not as if you're the only person who watches the television, listens to the radio, surfs the internet, reads the newspaper, and attended public school.

I ask—What uniqueness do you exercise when you're built with the same innate wants that everyone is built with? You too hunger, thirst, and desire to belong.

I ask—What's so unique when the popular culture and the collective intelligence induce the same behaviour and habits in all people? What's so unique about wanting what everyone wants—large amounts of cash, a few vehicles, status, respect, and a summer cottage?

I ask—What uniqueness do you exercise when each does as everyone else? So to fit in, you too chase a nine-to-five, the basics, the bills, a line of credit, a mortgage, entertainment, and the other elements of the accepted image?

They say that you and I can be individuals? They say that you and I have a uniqueness that we can exercise? They say... They say... They say... And I think they say so to destroy our true power. Only in unity can we usher in a higher living standard—the type that produces an enlightened people.

We should be treated as water, but we were melded into rock.

Starry-Eyed

Collective power is dead. Collective thought is blind. There is no wall dividing enslavement and mankind.

Pursuant to a few years of thought, a few broken hearts, and traveling outside the box and back in again, I realized that the artificial world and the rulers are to blame. The two stole our solidarity and the two stole our means to make change. Without solidarity and resources, no meaningful change can be made and the dark clouds will keep coming again and again.

You see, the machine subsists but we resist—we stand disunited and giveaway our strength. Unity is the only means to modify man's greatest instrument, public policy, and instil enlightenment. All the "big guys" are self-interested.

Natural Selections

We were designed to have wants and it's as natural as winter and fall. However, not all wants are born with us and most wants are limited constructs, given by our environments.

Yet, for some reason, there are those who strut as if they're infinite. Unaware, they select wants from a pool deficient. A pool filled and manned by the consumer culture and all its instruments.

Taught we were to want inside limits, and simultaneously, taught we were to think the pool we select from is bottomless.

Taught we weren't that the limited and predetermined wants found in the pool were created with a purpose. They guide us and create compliance.

This to ensure the supply-lines stay unravelled. This to ensure collective thought doesn't travel. Beliefs and wants constructed unguided can be unpredictable. Unwanted change can occur. The people might want more. Imagine a built world complimentary of the human creature.

....

There are those who believe the wants that drive their motions were natural selections. There are those who believe they exercised independence and freedom to construct the wants they're with. But the truth isn't what popular thought thinks it is and the facts are much more determined.

We can be trained differently but we were raised senseless. We were bred to overindulge and over-consume and to think it heaven sent.

Like an Island

The glove of ideology on the hand that wrote history graduated from the school of individuality and possession. As such, the glove's limited knowledge manifest has misled newer generations. Instilled is a limited perspective.

What I'm trying to communicate is that modern institutions and popular knowledge have transformed the human creature into an island—the kind that John, in his poem, *No Man is an Island,* suggested could not exist. But the fact is, people are disconnected from other humans.

"No man is an island, entire of itself.
Every man is a piece of the continent, a part of the main.
If a clod be washed away by the sea,
Europe is the less, as well as if a promontory were,
as well as if a manor of thy friends or of thine own were.
Any man's death diminishes me, because I am involved in mankind,
and therefore never send to know for whom the bell tolls,
it tolls for thee."

Sorry Mr. Donne, you too were working with limited knowledge. You too forgot to imagine the power of modern communications. The modern means to influence and shape a person's cognitive content and thought process are more advanced and more powerful than ever. And tragically, these modern means are employed to disconnect one from the other and mutate each into an island.

Some say that the world can never be a better place. Some say that the degradation can never be remedied.

I say—Teach the many differently and let us see. I say—Forget the consumer's identity and instruct the citizen's responsibilities.

Circumstances

Years went by as I gazed at the night canvas so to connect the shiny specks of dust. On an unknown number of occasions the sun bowed and the moon took its place—changes occurred beneath my feet—the grass grew above my waist. And almost every changing of guard brought with it notions unaligned to those built inside the popular crate, like the wisdom that revealed the nature of the human being.

Unfortunately, the revelation was a little depressing. After man mastered the ability to instil beliefs and wants within a person's value system, he inadvertently or purposely stole the greatest responsibility.

You see, if born amid diamonds, a person will translate and shine. If born orbiting, a person will translate and rise. If born in the air, a person will translate and fly. But born to the artificial hardships of the 21st century and the upside-down popular beliefs, a person is simply passing time before they die.

The temperament of the human creature is to become and to befall the environments around her or him. This is a truth no woman or man can outrun. Can someone please tell the people who rule the manmade world? Perhaps, if they know, they'll modify civilizations to fulfill a higher potential. One able to mould every person into a captain of their soul. All riddles aside, the human has the potential of a demi-god.

Dismantled, all that is me was given to me, and all that is me is constituted by my genes and metaphysical energy. With them, I gather from my surroundings, and with the three combined, my mind's community becomes and be. Accordingly, my value system is due to the three interacting, and my physical and cognitive motions are scripted by the three dancing.

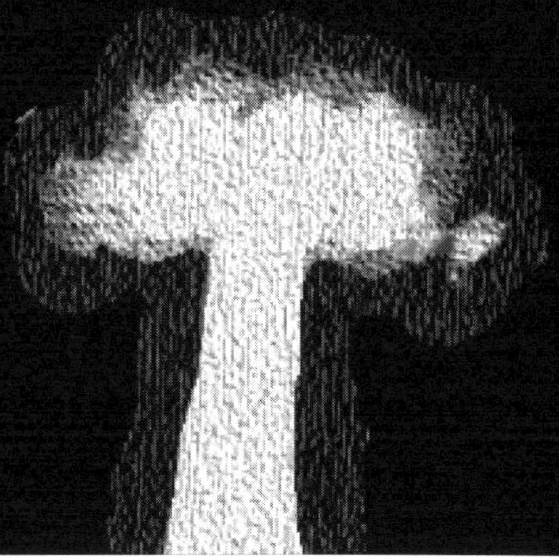

A Curse or a Blessing?

The design of my mind, and the knowledge I've gathered in the time I've been alive, have made it difficult opting into the ideas that present a challenge. Unable to opt out, I can't resist but pick up the pen and tie together words to make sentences.

Now, I wasn't looking to develop thoughts that challenge—for those who challenge only suffer—but that's where the knowledge I gathered led me, and once a person knows, it's unbecoming not to communicate the findings.

To endeavour to understand the truth is like sparring bare-knuckle with confusion, frustration, and pain, or like entertaining the feelings of Van Gogh the moment before his demise. But to understand is like dancing with the emotions of Einstein when he discovered mass and energy have a bond, and to understand is to conquer the material world without unsheathing the tempered blade or firing the cannons.

I was born with broken wings and stone feet. To make matters worse, I don't care much for shiny things. I'll concern myself with the earthly after the world changes. For now, I'll live as I was built to, under the dark clouds and battling the wicked—with the pen as my weapon.

Happiness

In my search for the state of consciousness known as happiness, I've hit many dead ends, or better put, many brick walls, and the first few I noticed only after leaving an imprint as Wiley Coyote typically does.

The brick walls I use as metaphors and to "wants" I actually refer. They've been the greatest obstacles in my search for happiness and they've been the cause of the sensations opposite.

A want hinders one's happiness by stimulating negative sensations. These sensations suppress the cognitive influences that produce happiness. A want can stimulate negative sensations on these occasions—when a want isn't satisfied, when the satisfaction is removed, and/or when the removal of a satisfaction is anticipated.

However, not all wants are perceived by the conscious mind and most act subconsciously, and a person isn't typically aware why the negative sensations surfaced. When this is the scenario, an individual will likely perceive the unsatisfied want as one with high value and purpose.

In accordance, it only makes sense to house fewer wants and those not easily unsatisfied. Wants constructed using such a formula are restricted in their potential to provoke negative sensations.

In my search for happiness I've hit many dead ends, or better put, many brick walls, and I'm still occasionally leaving an imprint. Although I understand cause and effect, it's easier said than practiced. Wants are not easy to control. Nevertheless, happiness beckons I endeavour.

Under Attack is the Happy Me

Unhappiness is good for the economy. Unhappy people tend to spend more money. Perhaps that's one of the reasons the market, through the culture of the consumer, readily attempts to influence a person's value system to house so many artificial, unneeded, and unrealistic wants. The more wants a person houses the greater the chance of dissatisfaction.

To Mimic

Pre-adults will mimic the behaviour of the people who appeal to their senses, and to mimic is a natural talent. Furthermore, a pre-adult can only mimic behaviour that he or she knows of, and this includes the knowledge he or she absorbs from the television, the radio, video games, and their parents.

Excluding the parents, the characters and the themes on television, radio, and in video games are unrealistic. And not only this, they're designed to appeal to the senses, and because they appeal, a pre-adult will naturally desire to mimic. As such, pre-adults are mimicking the messengers of sex, violence, vanity, and sensory pleasure.

...What?

Do you think I just make this stuff up? Have you heard how young adults talk about the opposite sex, not to mention their take on an injured pride and their idea of revenge? Why else do you think there are so many suburban 50 Cents and young Eminems? Why else do you think there are so many Lindsay Lohans and Paris Hiltons? Why else do you think "twerking" is stylish? And why else do you think there are so many middle-class boys who want to be gangsters?

Well, it's because they mimic and to mimic is a natural talent.

....

Bridled until the body's senses can no longer accept information, and the built world teaches to value the penchant. An excellent pupil by definition and the person is born innocent. To learn how morality is under attack, please read *Angel vs. Demon*.

As a rose was once a bud and a bud a seed, the human mind is no different and it too was sowed with the potential to be. But randomly sowed where it rains little and the sun rarely wakes, sometimes what grows is nothing more than a brittle and thorny stem, shouldering the potential to be. I ask—Is it still a rose or can I call it by another name?

Me

My thoughts and my actions are a product of the information I experience and amalgamate into my value system, and this information comes in many forms. The table my laptop is resting on—the buttons I'm pushing to make the words—the cup holding the coffee I'm about to pick up—the sensation of that coffee running down my throat—the person walking by and wearing a purple shirt—the articles in the newspaper resting next to my laptop—the dog chasing the cat outside the coffee shop—the song playing through the headphones—the red sports car that just rear-ended the grey Volkswagen—and the talk show on the television. It's all information.

Impressively, the human condition is designed to perceive, absorb, and manipulate external information, and the mind and body gather from every movement, event, surface, taste, scent, sound, and vibration, etc.

External information, in any physical or invisible form, is what the human condition is designed to absorb. In essence, information is what we were, what we are, and what we become—no matter the slightly unique manner each person is geared.

An Unbiased Mind

Unbiased at first, the mind is naturally attracted to most information. Information, negative or positive, consciously and subconsciously, influences the construction of values and the neural pathways that facilitate.

This process is natural. But did nature anticipate artificial attractions to grow and dominate? Did nature anticipate attractions such as the liquor, the gambling, the club scene, the X-rated TV, the popular image seen on the big screen, and the violent video games to grow so popular? And did nature anticipate their existence to appear so natural?

....

The mimicker naturally constructs neural pathways and those pathways will persuade a person to seek the artificial. Moreover, the search for satisfaction might be understood as a high value.

Popular culture manipulates a person's emotions as a painter manipulates color. More importantly, few are taught to master their emotions. Why? So to maintain and grow the status quo. An emotionally instable individual is easier to control, and a person in turmoil spends more.

The Caterpillar and the Cocoon

Crooked stems or rose petals?
Apple pies or rotten apples?

Degenerations within the extended womb,
the cocoon,
give refuge to caterpillars near bloom.
And if somehow they butterfly,
ugly is a guarantee,
as 1 plus 2 is 3.

And naturally,
when the societal structure is lacking,
lacking an enlightened psyche,
darkness will supersede beauty.

Popular media communicates messages that train the mind blind to the community, emanate immorality, and condition low-level beliefs such as the desire for shiny things. The evidence isn't hidden. Turn on the television or listen to the latest hip-hop hit and witness. There's so much contamination that it appears to have intention.

Unrecognized by our material lies, it hurts to see so many ignore the divine inside.

166

Bred This Way II

Material minded minion—like a combination of words without a comma or a period. Reincarnation is the end sentence.

And blame I do the givers of popular information. Popular media betrayed the person. Corrupt they do the moral intelligence.

Show and Tell

Known or not, a person's thoughts and actions are influenced by the information they absorb. So, it just might matter what the manmade world tells and shows. And if the built world only tells and shows half the information, only half the information will be absorbed. The outcome will be a person who knows only half the alphabet and lives in the land of sentences, words, and letters.

For some reason, popular media ignores the soul, and simultaneously, it trains a person to care little for the whole. Bred is love for the individual, and conditioned is the desire to chase artificially inflated wants and not those that carry higher value.

Trained to be... trained to be... perhaps, trained we be to reinforce the status quo. If not for our sweat, the world would not turn.

Raindrops

I feel your struggle inside. Do you feel mine? In such trying times and in a world of controlled lies, it's difficult not to question why the good is compromised.

And how did it get like this? In every community the degenerations exist and every generation has reached a new height in this.

Today's moral degradation didn't just spontaneously happen. Through all the conclusions reached, it was a slow process. Generations back, the clouds were contaminated.

The water cycle has cycled through innumerable times since, and the low and the dark clouds have hovered for generations—they've rained countless times on almost everything manmade.

An unknown number of cycles have cycled. The effect was naturally continual. Near all was polluted to one degree or another—everything social, political, spiritual, and economic.

The teachers of the people—the social, political, spiritual, and economic institutions—weren't prepared for the initial drizzle. Nor did they expect the monsoon that followed. Now, we're trapped in a polluted cycle perceived as natural. The degenerations long ago became factual. Infallible to one's rationale. Until a journey is taken outside the box, to a place above the low and the dark clouds, the clouds will remain perfect and indestructible. Sometimes it's necessary to look at the built world detached and as an outsider.

From the outside looking in I am, and a question naturally accompanies my travel back—How to filter out the degenerations so prevalent? Let me rephrase—How to improve the built world so a higher value system can be again developed?

After travelling outside the box and back in again, with my wits and intellect re-energized by the solar flares cast by the shadow of the Great Dragon, the one described by Hermes Trismegistus, an idea remains within the time and space of my thoughts and actions. To morally sweat is our only option.

Perhaps the rain will be kinder to the next generations. Maybe reincarnation is a Universal principle and it is we who benefit. Either way, it is one of the greatest secular purposes.

Trolls of Suffering and Pain

On this particular page of tomorrow's history, ideal conditions only half be, and sadly, I'll never see the places my dreams see. My mortal deficiencies prevent me from sitting with Guru Gobind's Warrior-Poets and Plato's Philosopher-Kings.

Nothing is gained by wanting social change. In today's day and age, against the grain, the trolls of suffering and pain become friends and enemies. But what else am I to do? It's the furthermost purpose. Besides, I'm forever built like this. It's in my cultural genetics—genes designed behind a veil of ignorance and given by The Spirit's consciousness. I have one ally and it's the Universe. Check the history, it's an anomaly. I was born starry-eyed and I will die standing. I ask— Is anyone else with eyes starry?

If you'd like to know more about Guru Gobind's Warrior-Poets, please read *Confessions: a lion's roar—a poet's war.*

Born Pure

Born pure but taken by the counterfeit cocoon. To the detriment of you and I, innocence accompanied our exit from the womb.

The quick exploitation of our innocence transformed into a bracelet of ignorance on each wrist, and each bracelet is chained to a steel ring around the neck.

But to be as Superman we can pretend. Hold tight the steel necklace with both hands, take a deep breath, and then apply stress. Look to unpopular knowledge as your sun to gain the strength.

Change seems hopeless and the truth inside us worthless. Alone, and with only a stick and a stone to battle with, how to move against the grain without resources?

Stick and Stone

May I ask—What type of books do you read? Do they touch why we breed? Do they discuss why we proceed in greed? Do they explain why knowledge is conditioned and constructed? Do they reveal why gladiators fell and mobs erupted? What if conditions were adjusted?

Imagine a higher state of awareness given by the machine. Imagine an environment which facilitates a rational cost to eat and be. Imagine a community soiled in morality—moral politicians, bankers, CEOs, priests, lovers, neighbours, friends, and family. Like the power of the seasons over a leaf, no more soap opera societies, artificial enemies, disunity, and abused technologies.

But change seem hopeless and the truth inside us worthless. Alone and with only a stick and a stone to work with, how to bring about change so to improve the human condition?

Perhaps if we grew to become more than male black-bears roaming the woods alone and more as a pride of lions working together, we might make change happen; defy we might the degenerations. We must stand together peacefully proclaiming "*audemus jura nostra defendere*".

To defend our rights we dare. For a better world we care. In the eyes of giants we stare. Imagine a billion stones and a billion sticks waved at the destroyers.

The Army of the Social Activist

The contemporary environments and the popular messages have bred within the contemporary person a weak social conscious. Far too many individuals care for the self and not the betterment of the whole. Disconnected they are. Not to mention that the attitude, 'someone else will take care of it', is a very popular state of mind—it ferments alongside the popular depiction of individuality. Very few people are without it, and very few people are standing toe-to-toe and eye-to-eye with the causes that are forcing a regression of civilizations. All this indicates that the army of the social activist is slowly dying.

The army of the social activist is dying because the newer generations are not enlisting and replenishing the ranks. Their minds are distracted by unrealistic and artificially inflated beliefs and wants. And those most socially active are now past their prime. With few left to stand guard, what hope is there for the yet born?

The Good Citizen

Corruption is all around us. The idea has infiltrated the highest of organizations. Examples are more than rampant. Examples are more than rampant but the good citizen remains blind, deaf, and silent.

And it's difficult to blame the good citizen. Disunited and with only the power of an individual, the overall system short-circuits a person's eyes, mouth, and ears. The right to Miri Piri is taken and few attempt to defend. And if a person does stand solo, he or she is at high risk of retaliation. Fortunately, before a person stands, an individual is typically slapped back into their seat by our poor socio-economic conditions. If a person does decide to stand toe-to-toe, he or she will most likely lose their employment and their means to pay the bills, feed their kids, keep a roof over the head, and maintain their social interactions. And let's not forget the depression, anxiety, and cognitive suffering the losses can induce. The good citizen is too often coerced to go along with the corruption.

What to make of all this? Even if a person was able to bring about a positive change, after their death, things might return to the way they were. What change can be made when the sheep are afraid to become shepherds?

....

Miri Piri—*The words were initially used together by the Great Guru Hargobind, and he symbolized the term with the two swords he carried. One sword symbolized "Miri" and the other symbolized "Piri". The term represents both earthly (Miri) and spiritual (Piri) authority. He believed that "Miri Piri" was the right of every woman and man and each should work to embody the term.*

To change our social contract is to challenge the few who rule, and to step to them is to brave the deepest pockets. Until we stand together under a righteous collective consciousness, all attempts will be soundly defeated. Until we stand together guided by the spirit of peaceful non-compliance, we will live and die never experiencing a higher living.

How to Change the World

Many individuals desire to improve the conditions the people exist in, and every generation, men and women effort toward this end. Yet, countless have come and gone and the status quo remains. This is so because those who desire a better world are trimming the branches and not pulling out the roots.

The roots are not unearthed and this is because the knowledge required to lift the masses above the artificial suffering induced by our current eco-political arrangement isn't taught, and most people who wish for a better world are not sacrificing to learn how to improve human existence.

Like a Shakespearean tragedy, tragically, the required knowledge is allusive, and no school is teaching this wisdom. A person must seek this knowledge without knowing where to begin the quest. To make the journey a little more hopeless, the knowledge is locked behind an unknown closed door, 50 feet thick, and guarded by 1000 armed men—metaphorically speaking. The task to learn how to make the world a better place and the causes of our hardship is Herculean. Yet, this is the duty of every living person—to discover why the world turns and how to turn it. With this understanding, a person might emancipate the planet, and with this understanding, a person has an opportunity to harmonize with heaven and live with true purpose. Without this awareness, does one truly live?

The New World: A Flower in February

The hands of time and circumstance temporarily made peace. In the process, they shook hands and gave birth to a place with the potential to be.

Why they finally came together is a mystery. Who knows? Perhaps it's a natural occurrence as the changing of seasons, a natural evolution. Or perhaps it's a fluke as life is to a scientist. Whatever the reason, one thing is certain... the New World's potential to be... to be an example.

An example of the next stage in humanity's evolution. One removed from war, poverty, illiteracy, and the degenerations of our contemporary history. One designed by peaceful, truthful, respectful, resourceful, and enlightened surroundings. These are the conditions required for the human creation to bloom and be.

To bloom... to bloom and be. Perhaps, as a summer flower in February, the New World is yet to bloom and be. To be… to be like Guru Gobind's Warrior-Poet or Plato's Philosopher King.

The New World is destined for greatness. Providence. F. Bacon's new Atlantis. This backwardness is simply the Old grasping at the power it once held. The attempt is futile. Fate is the gardener. The New will bloom, become, and fragrance the world.

.

....

We've advanced through so many stages—far beyond the days of hunting, gathering, tribes, chiefdoms, and monarchies. And let's not forget that decades were added to human living, automobiles and airplanes are the new donkeys, and galaxies far beyond ours can be seen. So, is it really that farfetched to think that our journey isn't at its end, and North America is yet to bloom and yet to release the perfect fragrance?

Age of the Aquarian

Although this era has its deficiencies, for the Age of the Aquarian to be, this epoch must first breathe. It's like a prerequisite.

Why? Well, for the Aquarian to be, the basic needs of all must be met with ease. Furthermore, the manmade world must be able to communicate enlightened knowledge to all humanity.

Ironically, the stage the world is currently in, and the type of human nature it invokes, is able to create technologies, knowledge, and an infrastructure with the ability to provide all people with the basics, and able to communicate an enlightened value system to all faiths and walks of life. When we begin to use this age's innovations for greater purposes, then we'll begin to move towards the next stage in our evolution.

Technology is a very important prerequisite. Without it, the knowledge required can't be effectively communicated to every person, and the appropriate value system can't be implanted within every individual.

Modern technologies have already demonstrated their abilities to effectively instil values, e.g., the consumer. The system has already proven the potential. However, the information required to enter the next stage of our evolution is missing or hidden.

....

Hope there is. Hope for the babies. Hopefully, they'll grow to do more than just consume things.

Will you join me on the battlefield? Will you fight with me to belong to the earth first? Or will you stand on the side lines and sacrifice the generations yet born to this curse.

Why Him?

Every other person desires to lead as Martin Luther King, Banda Singh, or John F. Kennedy did. But only a handful of people are willing to make the financial and social sacrifices to learn what the true roots of the problems are. For this reason, positive change is hard to come by—the intention is there but not the knowledge.

More importantly, too many are troubled when another person publicly voices their desire for change. In them arises hate and jealousy. "Why him?" And, "It should be me?" These are the two questions that provoke the animosity. These are the two questions that prevent unity.

The change this nation needs, in my lifetime, I might not see. There is just too much hate and jealousy amid the people who require and desire a better existence.

The New Romans We Be

Ironically and historically, when society evolves to provide a safe, stable, and resourceful environment, morality thins and compromise thickens. Oddly, when society reaches a point near truthful living, the crooked in the human condition surfaces, strengthening the crooked collective consciousness (ccc).

Why? I suppose at times we act more beast than enlightened—burnt Rome and Babylon we did and learnt we haven't. And again at the height of living modern living is—at a point near evolution we live—and again there is a choice.

Take a break from the chase and ask yourself one question—Do we embrace our potential or do we allow the ccc to grow?

The crooked collective consciousness is like the collective intelligence but crooked and it refers to the accumulation of all crooked thoughts and actions—thoughts and actions executed individually. Moreover, the word "crooked" means immoral and immoral divides into two: immoral thoughts and immoral acts. An immoral act is one that intentionally or unintentionally hurts a conscious existence by preventing the development or influence of the better parts of the mind, and an immoral thought is one that desires to hurt a conscious existence.

Trickling from the very top down, the crooked are everywhere—crooked politicians, CEOs, peacekeepers, neighbours, teachers, lovers, entrepreneurs, clergymen, and administrators. In every environment, institution, and corporation they breathe. Search your memories and you'll eventually see as me—the new Romans we be.

Will we repeat history and will we burn great cities (metaphorically)? Perhaps if we feed our popular culture and our collective intelligence enlighten information the people might translate and become enlightened. Perhaps then we might see how close we truly are to a greater existence. But who knows, maybe I've tripped and bumped my head against the ivory tower and knocked myself unconscious... again.

Unable to see the treasure within and unaware of the parts of the mind that separate us from all earthly creations... the highest Karmic manifestation... acting like monkeys had more divine purpose.

Adam Smith's Side-Effect

I heard truthful living is dead—I heard it took two to the head for the ends—I heard this from an old friend, liqoured again, as he was standing at the smoker's bend.

"We're enslaved to be slaves, you know what I'm sayin'." He said as he took another toke of his cigarette. *"We're enslaved because common beliefs stimulate mostly the selfish me, and to twist it a little bit, we're individually resourceless to change the things in need of change."* Inhaling and exhaling while speaking. *"To make the situation even more contemptuous, the people don't care to see a world different. It's difficult for them to let go of something the selfish within enjoys long enough to mimic a good citizen. It's like trying to convince a cocaine addict she's addicted or me to let go of this cigarette. It isn't happening over night."* Laughing, he threw his cigarette to the ground and walked into the club.

I remember him from Poli Sci 301. A very intelligent guy but something never stopped troubling him, and unfortunately, his escape from his mind was the rum. Although this time he mumbled most of his words, I still knew what he was talking about. He's lectured me before, and as then, he was trying to express a concept he called A.S.S, and looking outside at the line of people waiting to get into the club, I can't help but think he's onto something.

The first time he spoke of the concept was the first time we met. He and I were standing outside the lecture hall—late as usual—and listening to our professor through the space between the doors. The professor was quoting a passage from Adam Smith's book, *The Wealth of Nations*, when buddy looked at me and whispered, *"I read somewhere that Adam Smith once got his tongue stuck to a metal pole."* What he said caught me completely off guard and I looked at him like you would at a guy wearing high heels in a Catholic Church. But then my mind started visualizing Adam Smith stuck to a pole, in the middle of winter, and wearing a kilt. Why a kilt? Because Adam was Scottish and you know how the mind works—it fills the blanks to an incomplete picture.

Forgetting that the lecture hall was virtually silent, the professor exempt, and the fact that I was standing so close to the door, I started snickering and so did he. Comically, his snickering turned my snickering into a light laughter and my light laughter turned his. There's no better metaphor than a snowball rolling. As you can imagine, him and I were both leaned up against the door and holding our stomachs. By now, the lecture hall was silent—including the professor. Needless to say, we both turned and quickly made our way towards the nearest stairwell.

Outside we started talking some more—mostly about the information that was being covered in the lecture hall and this idea he called A.S.S. An idea coined to describe a population that's lost interest in a better world, act in agreement, and live in the pursuit of selfish ends. A.S.S—Adam Smith's Side-Effect.

The side-effect encompasses the myth of the Invisible Hand and Adam predicted that the best societal conditions would emerge if the individual and the market were free to pursue their own self-rational interests. Adam Smith was mistaken. The same forces that drive the free market also give life to the distractions, an underdeveloped value system, and the irrational cost to live. And keep in mind that if the machine wasn't in need of the degenerations, as the high cost to eat, they wouldn't exist. This according to the principles of the Invisible Hand.

Back to the principles at hand, I came to the club for the liquor, ladies, and lights, and not to realize I was wasting me. Although it was nice meeting an old friend, it probably wasn't the best time to meet one so prophetic. Don't get me wrong, what he said makes complete sense, but how to fight the mind? The weekends were spent senseless for years, brain patterns were developed, and value configurations were created. Meaning that the mind gave life to wants and habits and wants and habits are very difficult to destroy, especially when the selfish me is pleased by them.

What to do, what to do? Walk out or stick around and forget the thoughts induced? Outside and within, how to sacrifice and move against movements popular?

Either we change or "bang-bang"—two bullets to the head. We waste resources when we walk this dirt dead.

Caged

I have to daily remind myself that I don't function well in the maze. I also have to remind myself not to openly talk about the awkward disposition. Why? Well, one too many are busy looking for the cheese and they haven't stopped to realize that they're trapped in a maze. When the idea of a maze is introduced to their consciousness, they do little but laugh and hate.

And naturally, they were bred to think as mice in a maze. Born in the maze, taught to live and run around in the maze, and programmed to quietly die in the maze. They think the maze is a natural thing and this illusion is their conscious reality. When this reality is unveiled, to avoid cognitive dissonance, a person naturally laughs and hates.

The pain that comes when a dominant belief is challenged is a natural happening. As is the ability to surpass the threshold. People do it every day. People are daily overcoming their peak and I'm not the only living at this end of the bell curve. It would appear that more and more are joining what was once an exclusive club. More and more people are conceptualizing an image, deciding what paint and brush to use, and painting the picture for themselves.

To all the other mice who've realized that they're in a maze built inside a cage, I salute you, and I applaud your attempt at living. In this day and age, it isn't easy moving against the grain.

....

I was born with broken wings and stone feet. To make matters worse, I don't care much for what popular culture dictates I should be with such as a couple of kids, a mortgage, and the shiniest things.

I'll concern myself with them after the world changes. For now, I'll live as I was built to, under the dark clouds and on the earth they soften.

Trouble

If you haven't guessed, to my detriment and by the hands of Kismet, troublesome I've been. Troublesome I've been and labelled I was. Labelled a problem by those who can't see the invisible chains and the division of power.

Labels were given, and from the outside looking in, it might seem as if I'm not fully committed to our popular culture and our collective intelligence. From the outside looking in, the limited information can create a limited conclusion devoid of the knowledge that explains expectations and higher purpose. Why else would the labels exist? And perhaps the audience is unaware of the many times I've leaned and quietly listened—a side-effect of available hueristics.

Yet, know this my critics—The silence far outweighs the rebellions. Know this my critics—My obedience comes with prerequisites. And know this my critics—I follow ideas greater than the self. I can't reason giving my loyalty to ideas that distract and divide, and perhaps that's why I was labelled.

What will my tombstone read? 1) *He came, he saw, he lived as a billion men before him.*2) *He came, he saw, he changed the world.*

Your Unique Life Purpose

If there is a unique purpose for every single person, then that purpose must be imprinted within the human uniqueness. Nothing outside an individual has the potential to carry the same exclusive value, simply because any other person can also undertake the venture. There is nothing unique when many do the same. The only uniqueness each person is privy to is what's within the self.

Now, if the many saints of the past were correct, the sole purpose is to conquer the dark elements within, such as anger, lust, attachment, selfish ego, and greed. In this purpose, each is unique because each houses dark elements that influence at different degrees, and the more they influence the greater the struggle will be. No person will endeavour as another.

The rewards for completing the goal are many. The foremost are salvation and immortality. Immortality is possible but not of the physical.

Like a snowflake that never melts—like a tornado that doesn't swirl—like a lightning bolt fashioned in the workshop of an angel—the soul is more. The true "I" is built as a demi-god.

....

The past gave reason for the passion. The heavens gave meaning to the lies. From a whisper in a living wind, grows a glimmer in my eyes. And strive I do, through the chambers of my inner self. And claim the prize I do, the key to the door I'll face after the body falls.

Recognize the metaphysical surrounding our gated movements. You see, physical activities are not very sophisticated, nor are they the primary cause of motion.

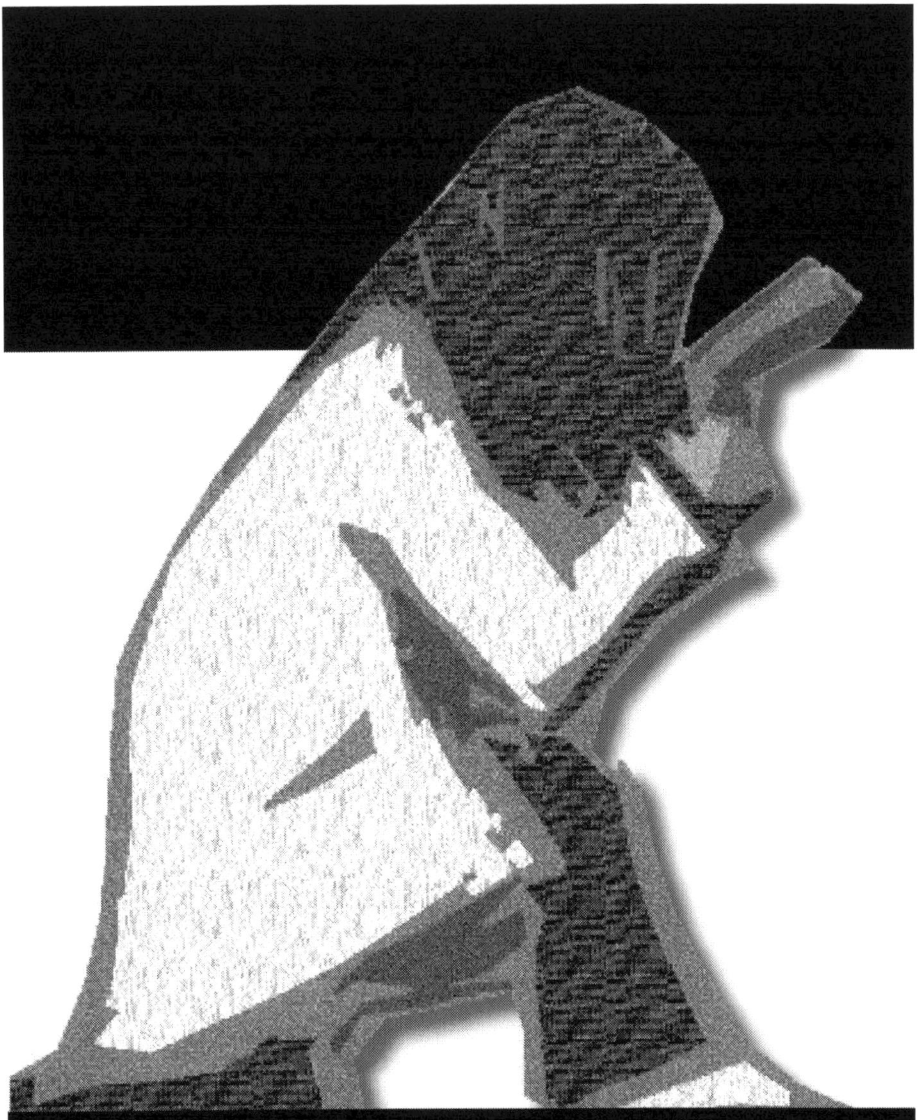

Lust, anger, the ego, attachment, and greed,
to conquer them is to live in harmony, and
to conquer them is to conquer the living.

Stardust in my Shoes

I've searched high and low for the remedy to enter me. I've searched high and low for the right frequency to be with me. I searched high to light my mind and energy. I searched low to know the dark in me.

All this I did for harmony. All this I did for the immortal me. All this I did and found I have stardust in my shoes, yellow in New Orleans' blues, water on the moon, and inside me a purpose higher than a consumer's.

The Same Caste

- All are the same if the mind blows in the wind and if death is perceived as the end.

- All are the same if detached from the higher mind and if the mind's eye is blind.

- All are the same if the soul isn't developed and if the ego envelops.

You can be a doctor, a waiter, or a judge. You can be a beggar, a junkie, or a thug. In the end, it doesn't matter under which title a person struggles. All are of the same caste if all do not attempt to conquer the self.

Three types of hunger internally influence the human condition, and they are the hunger generated by the body, the mind, and the spirit. To optimally function, a person must satisfy all three hungers.

Immortal Me

To reach.
To conquer.
To be immortal me.

This is a two part treaty.

The first is to see.
The goal is to reach.
There, where Ying and Yang meet.
There, where evil and good speak.
The time and space is ideal to see—
to see immortal meaning in me.

But only after one conquers the duality
will the immortal breathe.
This is a battle between "I" and me.
This is the latter half of the treaty.

To reach.
To conquer.
To be immortal me.

Lagoon

Imagine the plane of existence as an ocean, home to an island, and in the center of that island a lagoon. Imagine that every human life begins in this lagoon. Imagine that the purpose to life is to swim to land, travel across the island, and to live at the ocean's feet.

To swim is to first recognize the self and the two governing components—the body and the soul.

To journey through the island is to discipline the temporal and to allow the soul to dominantly speak to the time and space of thought.

To live at the ocean's feet is to live in equilibrium. Until the tide washes in and out, the purpose is to live.

....

Not knowing how to swim. Unaware of what a person is. Umbilical cord still attached. Every individual is born in a lagoon.

We are spiritual beings having a human experience and not vice versa. Think of the true self as a pilot, and the body, with its components such as the mind, as the jet.

The Invisible Leeching-Effect

"The leeches" symbolize all the negative beliefs, wants, behaviours, ideas, and habits that separate a person from their higher self. The "effect" refers to the act of them becoming a part of a person's cognitive content, and contributing to the creation of a person's perception.

When the leeches become, they have the potential to influence the creation of a person's awareness, and they influence thoughts like the impulse to breathe. Crystal meth junkies exhibit symptoms similar in theory—meaning that the leeches trap the mind in a cycle of un-mastered wants, inclinations, and internal communications. Most of which are impatient, self-centered, and self-destructive.

What I'm suggesting is that the leeches grow to propagate unneeded wanting, and the unneeded wanting will distract thoughts from considerations with meaning.

Most vulnerable are the youthful, before the mind is set in its ways, because a young individual is receptive to most information. Virtually and randomly, any type of value system can be instilled in them—any want, belief, idea, behaviour, and habit can be conditioned. The swim to woman or manhood can be difficult, and without protection and guidance, the leeches will attach. Without protection and guidance, a person can become half of what it means to be a woman or man. During the swim, a wise teacher is required, to shield against the leeches.

....

So many lives wasted not knowing the leeches be. Leech-less, we can be Philosopher-Kings. Or at least, more than what we're trained to be.

Salt

Where to begin?
How to remove the leeches?
Sadly, we can't rely on the corporation.
Tragically, we can't rely on the government.
Need salt but no one to give it.
Few are leech-less.
The salt is self-discipline.
The knowledge required is hidden.
No guidance before the mind is conditioned.
How to make the salt or find it?
Modern times prescribe it.
Self-administration.

The Lord of the Tenth Gate scripted, and there are battles designed for mystical lions, and there are battles designated for Maya's servants. As the Great Gobind, become a divine lion. My friends, step onto the foremost battlefield and take your place amid giants.

Fragrance and Thorns

In this Dark Age of Kali Yug, the epoch furthest from the Age of Truth, the challenge is to develop the mind's better parts and conquer the five plunderers—lust, anger, attachment, selfish ego, and greed.

This is an absolute—unchangeable as the invisible nature of wind—an act in the play that is existence. Look inside the self and allow truth, love, humility, and compassion to make thoughts and script actions. With the dust from the feet of the Saints, apply the paintbrush to the body-canvas and ink the mind-planet with enlightenment.

I don't want to live and die a lie. So sacrifice... I try... I live against the wind and pretend to fly.

Kismet and Me

Through genetics and as an architect, Kismet (fate) designed you and me, and most pertinent, Kismet designed our innateness. Likewise, we all house the same innate units. The only difference is that some are predisposed stronger in some than others. Some are weaker than another's. Some are completely silent. Some speak loud and others quiet. And some are out-and-out dominant.

Well, Kismet designed me to innately rebel. Kismet designed one or a few of my innate units to strongly influence my mind to challenge the status quo.

Wait, give me a minute here. Let me gather my stuff and step down from the pedestal.

Perhaps I wasn't built to defy. It might be that I view the built world differently because that viewpoint was accidentally indoctrinated within me by the elements of the world.

Or perhaps the innate units that trigger the challenge weren't born stronger in me than in another and they initially equally influence all people. However, it might be that if they aren't administered enough love and attention, and if constructed beliefs opposite to their nature grow stronger in presence, the influences of the innate units diminish.

Nonetheless, whatever the reason, I think it's safe to say that the manmade world was unable to construct ideas and beliefs within the likes of me to train the mind to stay in line.

The engineered collection of information that is our popular culture was incapable of overriding my intrinsic programming, so as to condition my mind to correlate, and unable to relate, it would appear I accidentally ignored the status quo and nurtured the difference.

Most would say it a curse. Some might say a blessing. The difference nurtured has made it near impossible to give-in to given meanings.

South Paw

For as far back as I can remember, I thought it was normal for the negative in the world to impact a person as much as it did me, and only recently have I begun to think differently. Only recently have I begun to identify the disability. If it was normal to be so sensitive to the human condition's suffering, then why aren't most people broken as me? Why aren't most coping with knuckles cut and bleeding? And why aren't most people challenging the elements that assault a moral society?

It might be that my mind's sensitivity is set to maximum and the warrior within is undisciplined. Or perhaps difficult circumstances everyone struggles with were multiplied by a dozen and this short manuscript is my unconscious attempt to conquer the mountains. It can only be the world or me and I'm not about to take full responsibility.

Most likely it's both. The way I was built and what the world dealt be two ends of a broken locket and they naturally attract each other.

Whatever it may be, the dye was cast and I be who I be. Built to challenge, built to be broken, and built to be rebuilt. But don't be fooled. Without the helping hand of friends and family, I'd still be in pieces, scattered on the ground.

I sense the tense coming of a new era and it's getting neara'. With each step I take, the Epoch becomes cleara'. But I must put my blacks on to cover the bags on my foolish futurist face procrastinating at a fast pace, as I release paper bullets and look toward the next Age.

The Changing Of Guard

With my feet up and a cold drink, it doesn't feel all that wrong to watch the changing of guard, and it doesn't feel all that wrong to gaze at the night stars.

I've been blessed in the sense that I didn't grow in an American ghetto, on a Canadian reservation, or in the middle-ages. There are no gunshots to waste thought on, no extremely poor socio-economic conditions that limit the parameters my thoughts are created within, and modern times prescribe no fall harvest to wake early for. Peace in mind has freed my time to watch the stars slowly reveal themselves, slowly compose themselves, and slowly share the stories only they can tell.

Last year, star gazing, they told the story of evil and good. They awoke an Eastern thinker who hugged me with his words and revealed the world behind the world. Mystically, inducing the truth above them both—describing hell as mortal and heaven on earth, and both as principles of the Universe.

This past month we went back to the Big Bang and they showed how they and "I" were distant family. After which, they helped me understand the "I" in me and showed how the "I" is actually three: chemistry, surroundings, and energy.

Two nights ago they extended their hands and pulled me up to sit with them. Through the eyes of a star, Muslims, Christians, and Hebrews prayed together in Jerusalem. We must've time traveled. And although there were brief periods in time when they all sat together, I'm hoping at tomorrow we marvelled.

And last night I saw the most incredible. I saw harmony on earth, a peaceful transformation of those who destroy her, a culture of the Philosopher King and the Holy-Trooper, a people who love The One

Eternal Creator, and benevolent eco-political leaders.

Incredibly just stars to some. Just twinkles of dust on a black canvas. But to men and women as me, they are gateways to the imagination and the heart. To men and women as me, they are the stuff worthy of thought. With my feet up and a cold drink, it doesn't feel all that wrong to watch the changing of guard, and it doesn't feel all that wrong to gaze at the night stars.

LOVE
BE LOVED
LIVE

59046473R00130

Made in the USA
Columbia, SC
29 May 2019